CYNDY SZEKERES'
I Love My
BUSY
BOOK

About the Alphabet, Counting, Colors,
Opposites, Shapes, and Much, Much More!

SCHOLASTIC INC. Cartwheel B·O·O·K·S®

New York Toronto London Auckland Sydney

Library of Congress Cataloging-in-Publication Data

Szekeres, Cyndy.
    [I love my busy book]
    Cyndy Szekeres' I love my busy book.
        p.   cm.
    Summary: A tiny mouse dances his way through this book of A,B,Cs,
1,2,3s, colors, opposites, shapes, animal sounds, feelings, and more.
                ISBN 0-590-69195-3
    [1. Mice—Fiction. 2. Alphabet. 3. Counting. 4. Color—Fiction.] I. Title.
PZ7.S988Cyke   1997
[E]—dc20   96-7438
                                                                        CIP
                                                                        AC

12 11 10 9 8 7 6 5 4 3 2 1   7 8 9/9 0 1 2/0

                    Printed in Mexico   46

            First Scholastic printing, March 1997

Table of Contents

Good Morning!

The sun is up,
and so are Frog, Chipmunk, and Mrs. Mouse.
Newt reads the news, Bird finds a worm,
while Woodchuck cleans her house.
Little Mouse finds berries;
his friends all laugh and play.
Bugs and spiders run about.
What a busy day!

Count: **3** spiders
1 worm   **4** ants
2 bees   **5** ladybugs

Rhyming Mice, Very Nice!

A,B,Cs

1,2,3s

Busy bees!

Eating cheese

Don't sneeze!

Planting peas

Hiding, seeking

Covering, peeking

Short

Tall

Big

Small

Hello!

Goodbye!
I fly my tie

9

We All Dress Up

Black hat,
how about that?

Brown shoes,
come in twos.

White shirt,
covered with dirt!

Blue tie,
catches your eye.

Purple socks,
with little clocks.

Pink pants,
make me dance.

Green jacket,
quite a racket!

Orange vest,
the very best.

Gray cape,
a silly shape.

Yellow bows,
for dainty toes.

Red cap,
good for a nap.

Who Has Good Manners?

I stay in my seat
while I'm eating.
— *Good Goat*

I don't speak
when my mouth is full.
— *Happy Hog*

If I have an accident,
I say, "I'm sorry."
— *Polite Puppy*

12

We use a special word
when we ask for something...
PLEASE!
— *Mannerly Mice*

...and, when we are
given something.
THANK YOU!
— *Caring Kittens*

We always share.
One for you,
one for me.
— *Behaving Bunnies*

When I leave the table,
I say, "Excuse me."
— *Cheerful Chipmunk*

If I don't want any,
I say, "No, thank you."
— *Outstanding Owl*

What Do the Animals Say?

One young pig in a fuzzy wig.
OINK!

Two fine dogs, one small, one big.
WOOF! WOOF!

Three downy ducks with curly tails.
QUACK! QUACK! QUACK!

Four sleek cats in gowns and veils.
MEOW! MEOW! MEOW! MEOW!

They took a stroll with five sweet mice
in satin vests that looked so nice.
SQUEAK! SQUEAK! SQUEAK! SQUEAK! SQUEAK!

It thundered and began to rain.
BOOM! SPLASH! BOOM!

And so they all went home again.
BYE-BYE!

Each went to bed, so it is said.
SHH-H-H-H!

But somebody is still awake!
A mouse who says…

"I WANT SOME CAKE!"

Do You Know Your A,B,Cs ?

Aa
Angry Angelo
argues with ants

Bb
Big Beverly
boils broccoli

Cc
Clever Christopher
crushes cupcakes

16

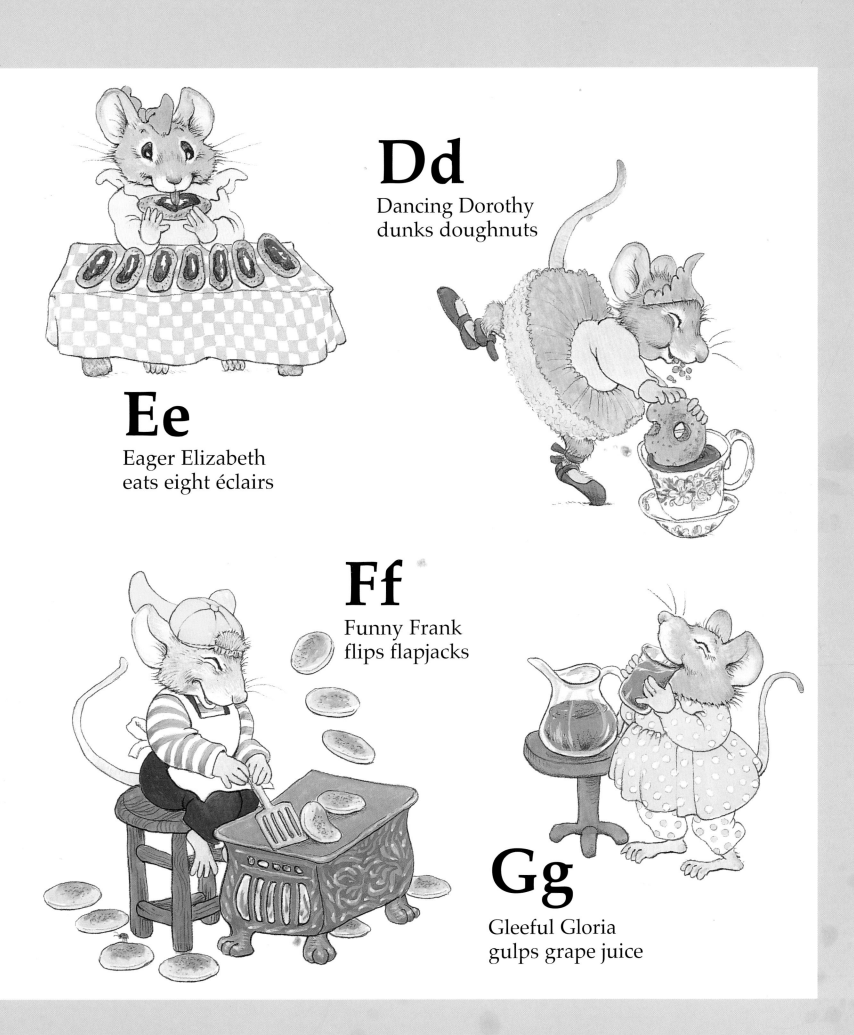

Dd
Dancing Dorothy
dunks doughnuts

Ee
Eager Elizabeth
eats eight éclairs

Ff
Funny Frank
flips flapjacks

Gg
Gleeful Gloria
gulps grape juice

17

Hh

Happy Harriet
hugs Henry

Ii

Impossible Imogene
irons ice cubes

18

Jj
Jolly Jeremy
jellies Joseph

Kk
Kindly Karen
keeps kissing Kevin

L l Lovely Linda
licks lollipops

Mm Magnificent Marco
munches macaroni

Nn
Noisy Nina
needs noodles

Oo

Older Ophelia
orders oatmeal

Pp

Picky Peter
prefers popcorn

Qq
Quibbling Quincy
quarrels with Quentin

Rr
Rowdy Roger
rides a rooster

Ss

Silly Susan
sings songs with Sylvia

Tt Timid Timothy
talks to toy turkeys

Uu

Unusual Ursula
unloads Uncle Ulysses

Vv

Vexed Victor
vacuums Vanessa

Ww

Winking Wilhelmina
waltzes with Walter

Xx

Excited Xavier Xs
xylophones

Yy

Youthful Yolanda
yanks yarn

Zz

Zany Zenobia
zigzags through
zinnias

Count the Busy Mice

1 mouse lighting candles
2 mice laughing
3 mice licking frosting
4 mice singing
5 mice tooting horns
6 mice dancing
7 mice peeking at presents
8 mice cheering
9 mice pushing
10 mice pulling

Happy birthday, Piggy Pig!

28

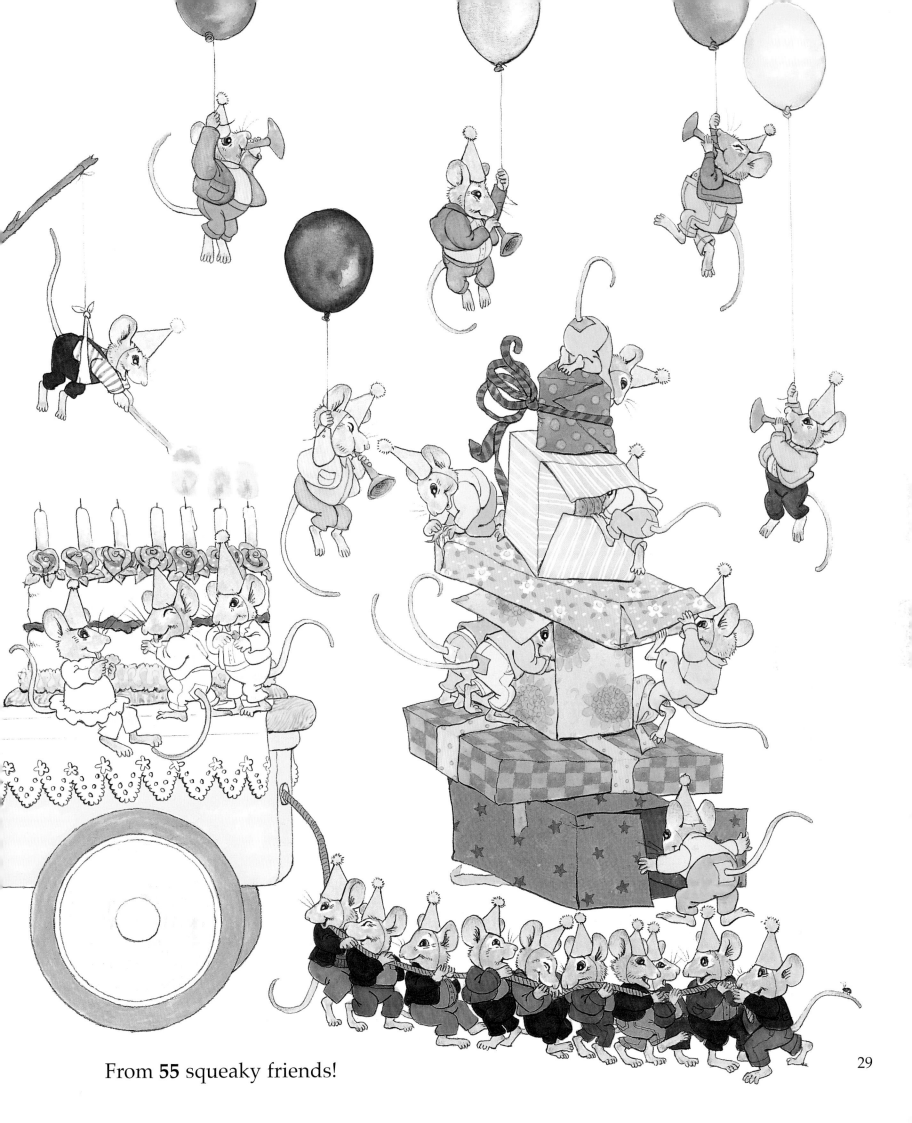

From **55** squeaky friends!

Shapes and Colors

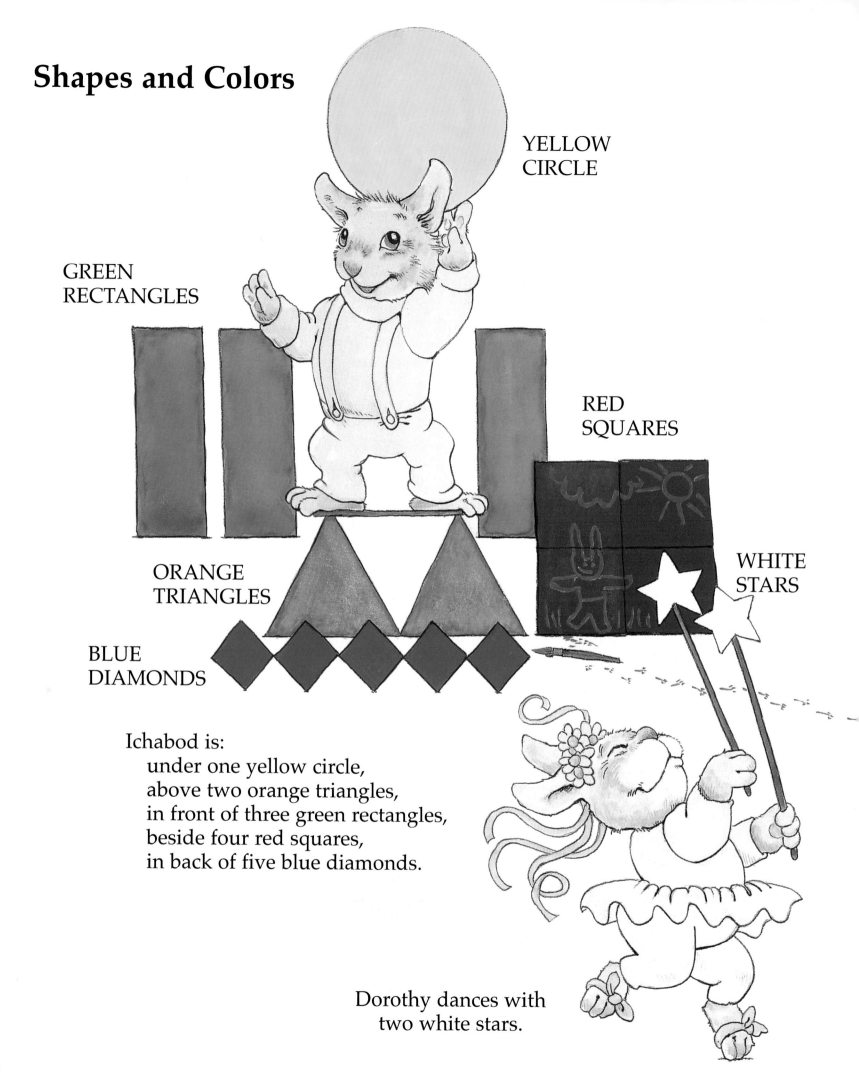

YELLOW
CIRCLE

GREEN
RECTANGLES

RED
SQUARES

ORANGE
TRIANGLES

WHITE
STARS

BLUE
DIAMONDS

Ichabod is:
   under one yellow circle,
   above two orange triangles,
   in front of three green rectangles,
   beside four red squares,
   in back of five blue diamonds.

Dorothy dances with
two white stars.

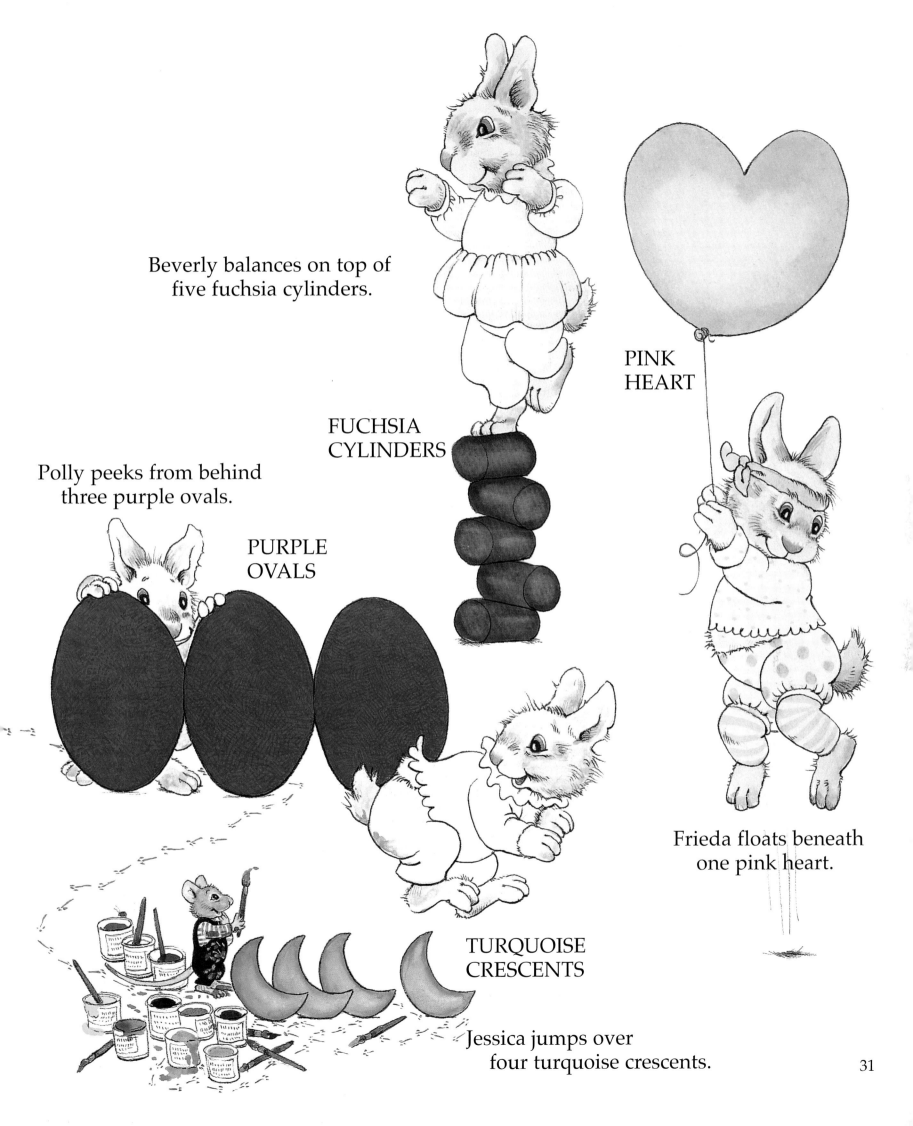

Beverly balances on top of
five fuchsia cylinders.

PINK
HEART

FUCHSIA
CYLINDERS

Polly peeks from behind
three purple ovals.

PURPLE
OVALS

Frieda floats beneath
one pink heart.

TURQUOISE
CRESCENTS

Jessica jumps over
four turquoise crescents.

31

How Do You Feel Today?

"See my happy face?" Little Mouse says, as he wiggles his whiskers with glee.

"I can look sad," quacks Duck in reply. "You will sigh with a tear when you see."

"I can look fussy... and mussy... and MAD!"

"I can do that! I can even look BAD!"

"How about scared,
or a look of surprise?"

"Just open your mouth,
make very big eyes."

"See this silly face!"
"Mine is the best!"

Two faces look sleepy.
Time for a rest.

I Can Do It!

"I can do it!" laughed Bunny,
as he zipped his zipper up.

His friend smiled. "I'm all buttoned."
What a clever little pup!

"This won't tie," complained Kitty.
Mouse said, "I shall do it for you."

"Dress yourself," said Chick to Duckling.
"Your mother will adore you!"

"We can do it, and we did it!"
sing six happy little friends.

Zippered, buttoned, tied, and tucked in.
So, this busy story ends.

My Body

Ears

Head

Neck

Arm

Eyes

Nose

Mouth

Teeth

Hand

Tail

Tummy

Heel

Leg

Foot

Toes

I am lots of parts and pieces,
I can show you, wait and see.
Head and body, arms and legs,
all together, they make me!
Eyes to see with,
nose to smell with,
and I listen with two ears.
Through my mouth, I fill my tummy
with toast until it cheers!
My arms and hands can carry toys,
my legs must carry me.
When music plays
my legs will dance,
and I'll sing merrily!

Up, Down, and All Around

Up is the ceiling,
down is the floor.
Left is the window,
right is the door.

In is the kitty,
out is the dog.
Over sleeps a little mouse,
under sleeps a frog.

Front, back,
clickety-clack

High, low,
away we go!

Small, big,
jiggety jig

Short, tall,
don't fall

Bottom, top,
I want to stop!

39

Bear Bike

Puppy Plane

Kitty Car

Turtle Truck

40

Things That Go

Wolf Wagon

Toad Train

Mouse Motorcycles

Squirrel Skateboard

Butterfly Boat

What Rhymes With Good Night?

Dog fight

Hold tight

Tail light

Make a kite

What a fright!

Out of sight

Be polite

Remember to write

Pillow fight!

Sleep tight

44

Bedtime

Who's in the tree hollow,
all cozy and warm?

Who sleeps under roots,
where he'll come to no harm?

Who is snuggled and snoring,
'neath a roof made of moss?

Who nests in the leaves,
where they'd better not toss?

Can you see someone sleeping
beneath the tree bark?

In a snug, sandy burrow,
who's there when it's dark?

Where's a fine feathered nest?
Is there someone still peeping?

When it's time for your slumber,
where do you go for sleeping?

Answers: owl; mouse; chipmunk; squirrels; ladybugs; bunnies; birds; bed!

One page
to dance on...

just for me

...and I do!

Because
I am special,
exactly
like
you.